The World's Greatest Valentine

by **Terry Collins**

illustrated by **Mark O'Hare**

Simon Spotlight/Nickelodeon

New York   London   Toronto   Sydney   Singapore

chapter one

"Happy Valentine's Day, Bikini Bottom!" With this jaunty cry SpongeBob SquarePants sprang out the front door of his pineapple home and ran across the ocean floor.

SpongeBob had thought February 14 would never arrive! His skinny arms were overflowing with valentines of all shapes and sizes. After weeks of waiting, he could deliver his custom-made gifts at last!

"First stop, a valentine for my favorite

next-door neighbor!" SpongeBob said with a happy giggle.

Dancing across the sea grass on the tiptoes of his shiny patent leather shoes, SpongeBob lobbed a large pink valentine into the lap of his frowning neighbor, Squidward.

"Happy Valentine's Day, pal!" SpongeBob sang. "Will you be mine?"

Squidward scowled, then sat back in his outdoor lounge chair. "Why don't you go play in shark-infested waters?" he suggested sarcastically.

"That's a great idea! Sharks need love too, and I've got lots more valentines to give!" SpongeBob replied with a wave. "Good-bye!"

"Good riddance," Squidward said sourly, shredding his valentine into confetti and tossing the pieces over his head.

Spotting Mrs. Puff behind the steering wheel of her blue-and-white motorboat, SpongeBob ran up alongside her vehicle.

"Happy Valentine's Day, Mrs. Puff!" SpongeBob called as he tossed her a red valentine with white lace.

"Oh, my! Thank you, SpongeBob!" the flustered blowfish replied as she opened the valentine.

"I get a bang out of you," Mrs. Puff read, not paying attention to where she was going. . . .

Crunch! Mrs. Puff drove right into a fire hydrant!

Pwooosh! Her body inflated to four times its normal size!

Luckily, Mrs. Puff wasn't injured thanks to her "built-in" air bag!

SpongeBob didn't hear the wreck. He was already dropping off another valentine.

Taking out a pair of tweezers, he selected the smallest paper heart from his pile and held it

out to a tiny green creature with one bulging red eye.

"SpongeBob!" the evil Plankton cried as he looked up. "So, Mr. Krabs has sent you to destroy me! Well, I'm ready for you! Give me your best shot!"

"Okay!" SpongeBob agreed. "Here you go!"

Plankton took the offering and read the note aloud. "I'd walk the plank for you! Be my valentine! Love . . . SpongeBob?"

"Ha-ha-ha-ha!" SpongeBob tittered as he skipped away. "Happy Valentine's Day, Plankton!"

"Curse you, SpongeBob!" Plankton boomed, hopping up and down with anger. "Curse you!"

SpongeBob wasn't listening. He continued dropping off valentines throughout Bikini Bottom. But he had to hurry, for there was a final stop to make before his Valentine's Day was complete. . . .

chapter two

SpongeBob arrived at Sandy Cheeks's underwater treedome. He was ready and eager to take his Valentine's Day plans to the next level.

Sandy was waiting outside in her white diving suit. She had a smile on her face and her hands behind her back.

"Happy Valentine's Day, SpongeBob! I'm nuts for you!" Sandy said with a grin as she handed over a heart-shaped acorn with a twig arrow through the center.

"And I'm bubbles for you, Sandy!" SpongeBob replied, taking out his bubble wand and a bottle of chocolate syrup.

A master of bubble blowing, SpongeBob blew a heart-shaped chocolate surprise to Sandy.

"Mmmm! Mighty tasty!" she said, gobbling up the gift through a portal in her air helmet. "Patrick's going to love the one you made for him!"

Together, SpongeBob and Sandy turned to look at the tremendous chocolate balloon tied down behind the treedome. The balloon was large enough to carry two people in the hanging basket below. There was even a pink marshmallow starfish attached to each side!

"Take me through the plan again," Sandy said as she examined the balloon. SpongeBob dipped the bubble wand into the syrup bottle, took a deep breath, and blew out a floating, three-dimensional chocolate model of the Bikini Bottom Valentine's Day Carnival!

"Step one: Patrick and I get to the Valentine's Day Carnival," SpongeBob said in a commanding tone of voice. "Step two: I position Patrick and myself on top of the Ferris wheel."

"Check and double check," Sandy replied, nodding in agreement. She was amazed at the detail of the chocolate model that hovered in the water.

SpongeBob blew a small bubble replica of the mammoth heart-shaped chocolate balloon. The replica floated over the top of the model carnival. "Step three: You arrive with Patrick's valentine at the designated checkpoint for maximum visual contact."

"Got it!" Sandy agreed, readying herself for take-off.

The small bubble landed on the boardwalk of the chocolate carnival. "Step four: Patrick is thrilled! Mission accomplished!"

"Sounds good, SpongeBob!" Sandy said, untying the ropes that held Patrick's Valentine's Day gift to the bottom of the ocean. "Keep me posted on the shell-phone."

"Right!" SpongeBob replied. "I'll go grab Patrick right now and Operation Valentine will be in full play!"

SpongeBob looked up proudly as Sandy floated away in the balloon. He could hardly wait to see the look on Patrick's face. This was going to be a Valentine's Day his starfish pal would never forget!

chapter three

Crunk! Crunk! Crunk! Crunk!

Patrick Star was breaking rocks.

Crunk! Crunk! Crunk!

One rock, actually. He was chipping the stone into the shape of a heart. Patrick knew SpongeBob would be arriving soon, and he wanted to have his gift finished.

Crunk! Crunk!

Patrick loved Valentine's Day almost as much as SpongeBob. The starfish had *even* bought a new white T-shirt with a red heart on the front for the occasion.

Crunk!

"There!" Patrick said, pleased with his handiwork. "Nice and smooth!"

The starfish lifted the stony valentine just as SpongeBob came up behind him.

"Hi, Patrick!" SpongeBob said.

Patrick looked confused. He peered down at the rock. "Hello?" he said.

"Patrick, it's me. SpongeBob," SpongeBob said.

"Oh, my gosh!" Patrick yelped, dropping the rock in shock. "SpongeBob's stuck inside this rock! Hold on, buddy! I'll get you out!"

Grabbing a second stone, Patrick began to smash the heart-shaped rock. With a series of hammerlike blows, he reduced the valentine to a pile of pebbles!

Patrick was horrified! Had he crushed his best friend?

"SpongeBob?" he whispered, sifting through the remains.

Standing behind Patrick, SpongeBob rolled his eyes. "Yes, Patrick?"

"SpongeBob! Oh, no!" Patrick said, falling to his knees and weeping. He picked up the rubble and held it to his cheek. "My poor pal!"

"Uh, Patrick? I'm right behind you!" SpongeBob said.

Patrick turned and leaped up with delight! "There you are!" he said happily, thrusting out the handful of pebbles. "Happy Valentine's Day! Here's your present!"

SpongeBob took the debris. "Thanks!" he said, then pointed at Patrick. "And I have a present for *you*."

Patrick's eyes widened with excitement!

"You do?" he said. "For *me!*"

"For you!" SpongeBob giggled. "It's the greatest . . . "

Patrick's eyes bulged. He tried to speak, but all he could say was, "Uhhh!"

SpongeBob continued, "The bestest . . . "

A trickle of drool ran down the side of Patrick's mouth. "Yeah?" he said.

"The most fantabulous . . . "

Patrick turned multiple cartwheels with anticipation. "UH-HUH! UH-HUH!"

"The single most amazing present . . . EVER!"

"EEEEEEEEEEE!" Patrick squealed, rolling around on the ocean floor.

"But," SpongeBob added in a teasing tone, "you can't have it yet."

"Huh?" Patrick hopped to his feet and thrust his face into the tip of SpongeBob's long nose. "Why not?" he asked in a hurt voice.

SpongeBob shrugged. "Because it's not ready yet."

Patrick paused for approximately one second. "Is it ready now?" he asked.

"Not yet," SpongeBob teased.

Patrick gritted his teeth. "Now?" he asked hopefully.

"Nope."

"How about now?" he asked.

SpongeBob put his hands on his square hips and frowned. "Do you want to ruin the surprise?" he asked.

"YES!" Patrick said, nodding his head up and down so that the water swirled around his neck like a miniwhirlpool!

"Ah-ah-ah-ahhh!" SpongeBob scolded, wagging a finger.

"Come on, please!" Patrick begged.

SpongeBob crossed his arms. "Sorry."

Patrick fell facedown on the ground. "You gotta tell me!" he pleaded.

"No can do, old chum. You'll just have to wait," SpongeBob said, struggling to move. He looked down at his feet. Patrick had locked both hands onto SpongeBob's right ankle.

"Please, please, please!" Patrick begged, hanging on for dear life as SpongeBob slowly dragged him toward the carnival.

"Uh-uh," SpongeBob said. "You know what they say . . . good things come to those who wait!"

"B-b-but . . . I'm tired of waitin'!" Patrick shrieked. "I want my present now!"

chapter four

SpongeBob glanced at his watch. He was making slower time than anticipated, as Patrick was still clinging to his ankle. He didn't want to be late and miss Sandy's arrival.

"Please! Please! Puh-leeeeze?" Patrick whined.

SpongeBob shook his leg, but his friend had a firm grip. He sighed and kept walking.

"PLEASE! Oh, please tell me! Please! Please?" Patrick begged. "Oh, please you gotta tell me! Tell me! Tell me! Tell me!!! . . . PLEASE!?!"

"Okay, Patrick! Here we are!" SpongeBob finally announced. "One surprise coming up!"

The starfish gazed out across the seascape and gasped. His mouth dropped open and he jumped for joy!

"You got me a carnival!?" Patrick cried happily as he raced through the entrance. "A carnival for me?"

"No, not a carnival, I mean, not exactly. . . ." SpongeBob said, trying to explain. But Patrick wasn't listening.

"Mine! Mine! Mine!" Patrick yelled, glowering at the other Bikini Bottom residents enjoying the attractions. "All right! Everybody out! This is *my* carnival!"

SpongeBob tapped Patrick on the shoulder. "It's not your carnival."

Patrick sagged. "Oh," he said.

SpongeBob dug into a pocket of his square

pants and took out twenty-five cents. "Here," he said, handing the coin to Patrick. "Why don't you take this quarter and—"

"Oh, my gosh . . . a QUARTER!" Patrick cried as he snatched the money from SpongeBob's outstretched hand. "I've always wanted a quarter!"

SpongeBob slapped his soggy forehead. "It's not the quarter," he replied.

"It looks like a quarter."

"It *is* a quarter, but that's not the surprise," SpongeBob explained.

"Oh," Patrick said. "Sorry."

"What I want you to do is take that quarter and buy some cotton candy," SpongeBob said, pointing to a small display cart on wheels. "And then—"

"COTTON CANDY! I can't believe it!" Patrick said, running toward the candy salesman with a wild-eyed look. "Gimme that cart! I'm claiming what is mine!"

The poor salesman ran for his life as Patrick chased him down the boardwalk.

SpongeBob giggled. Patrick was going to be thrilled when Sandy arrived with his surprise!

"Help! Get away! Help me!" the salesman yelled.

"Cotton candy! Gimme!" Patrick replied.

A burst of static erupted from SpongeBob's back pocket. He took out his shell-phone and pressed a button.

"Sandy to SpongeBob . . . come in, SpongeBob!" Sandy's voice crackled from the shell's speaker.

"SpongeBob here."

Onboard the chocolate valentine balloon, Sandy looked out across the ocean and spied the blinking lights and colorful flags of the carnival.

"I've got a visual on the carnival," she said. "You want me to bring 'er in?"

SpongeBob grinned. "Not yet, Sandy. Patrick's still trying to guess what his valentine is!"

Back in the gondola of the balloon, Sandy snickered. "You are such a kidder! Sandy over and out!"

She reached over and adjusted one of the guidelines, letting the chocolate balloon float in place.

Suddenly, she heard a chattering sound!

"Oh, no!" she gasped. A swarm of chomping shellfish was diving straight for the balloon! "Scallops!"

The situation got even worse.

As they got closer, Sandy recognized this particular breed of shellfish. "Chocolate-eatin' scallops!"

chapter five

Tired of chasing the cotton candy cart, Patrick paused in front of SpongeBob. "So, that wasn't my valentine?"

"Nope!" SpongeBob said.

"Then, what? What is it?" Patrick demanded. "I CAN'T TAKE THIS WAITING!"

"You'll have to guess," SpongeBob said with a chuckle.

Patrick ran over and pointed at the "Read Your Fin" fortune-telling tent. "This tent?" he asked.

26

"Wrong!" SpongeBob said. "You gotta try harder than that!"

Patrick grabbed a very surprised sea bass by the collar. "This guy?" he asked.

"Sorry, no!" SpongeBob said, struggling not to laugh.

Disgusted, Patrick hurled the sea bass away like a javelin and snatched a hotdog from one of the eight hands of an octopus.

"Hey! That's my lunch!" the octopus complained.

"How about this hotdog?" Patrick demanded.

"Tee-hee!" SpongeBob laughed. "Is that your *final* answer?"

Patrick pondered for a few seconds. "Yes," he said.

"No!" SpongeBob replied.

Patrick shoved the hotdog into the owner's mouth and raced over to the Valentine's Day science booth. Hunching over a microscope, he peered into the eyepiece and spotted a swimming creature invisible to the naked eye.

"This paramecium?" Patrick demanded.

SpongeBob held firm. "Sorry, no."

Patrick skidded to a stop and placed a friendly arm around SpongeBob's shoulders. "Heh, heh, heh. You're a sly one," he said with a crazed gleam in his eyes.

Then, the gleam brightened.

Patrick had an idea!

"If I can't find it here at the carnival, then it must be outside on top of . . . Mount Climb-Up-And-Fall-Off!" Patrick cried, racing out of the exit toward the nearby mountain range.

SpongeBob watched his friend grow smaller and smaller in the distance. Patrick ran to the top of the mountain and leaped off with a cry of "AAAAIIIEEE!"

There was a faint *thud* when he landed.

The fall didn't even slow the starfish down. He ran back to SpongeBob.

"The valentine . . . it wasn't there . . . either," Patrick gasped, trying to catch his breath.

SpongeBob's eyes narrowed. "Are you sure?" he asked.

Patrick considered this.

"Dahhh!" he yelled, then turned and ran all the way back to the mountain!

As SpongeBob watched Patrick repeatedly climb up and fall off the tip of Mount Climb-Up-And-Fall-Off, his shell-phone chirped.

"Hello?"

"Sandy to SpongeBob!"

"Roger, Sandy!" SpongeBob said. "You can bring the balloon in now!"

"Um, no can do, SpongeBob," Sandy replied.

Back at the heart-shaped balloon, the

squirrel was using all her kung fu fighting skills to hold the swarm of scallops at bay!

"Why not?" SpongeBob asked.

"We've got ourselves a little problem," Sandy replied, swinging out with a side kick to knock away a hungry shellfish. "Hi-yah! I got a pack of chocolate-eatin' scallops trying to rustle the balloon!"

chapter six

SpongeBob listened in horror. He could hear Sandy grunting with exertion as she battled the attacking scallops!

"Git away, ya sweet-toothed varmints!" she cried. "Hi-yah! SpongeBob, I'm gonna be a little late for the shindig!"

SpongeBob's entire body sagged in his clothes. "Late?" he said worriedly. "But what about—"

"AAAIIIEEE!" Patrick screamed, plunging

once more from the top of Mount Climb-Up-And-Fall-Off.

"Patrick?" SpongeBob finished in a hushed voice.

"Take him up on the Ferris wheel like you planned and I'll meet you there—I hope! Sandy over and out!"

SpongeBob put away the shell-phone. What was he going to do? If Patrick didn't get his valentine, there was no telling what he might do.

"I'm pretty sure it isn't up there," Patrick announced with a wheeze.

"Gahh!" SpongeBob cried in surprise. He hadn't heard his friend come back.

Patrick was a mess. The starfish's new white T-shirt was dirty, his hands were scuffed from the repeated dives, and his face was weary.

"Where . . . is it?" Patrick pleaded, gasping for breath. "Where . . . is . . . my . . . valentine?"

SpongeBob winced, crossed his fingers for luck,

and said, "Actually, it's on the, um, Ferris wheel."

"FERRIS WHEEL!" Patrick bellowed, grabbing SpongeBob by the hand and pulling him toward the brightly lit attraction.

Luckily, there wasn't a line and SpongeBob was able to buy two tickets for the ride. Patrick was entranced as the wheel slowly started to turn. He kept repeating over and over in a whisper, "Ferris wheel, Ferris wheel, Ferris wheel."

As they rose higher and higher, SpongeBob looked around anxiously for Sandy and the chocolate valentine balloon. Unfortunately, he saw nothing but deep blue seawater.

The wheel rotated to a stop. Patrick and SpongeBob were now in the tip-top Ferris wheel car, the highest spot in the carnival.

Patrick turned to SpongeBob. "I'm ready!" he said with a big smile. "I'm ready for the neatest valentine present in the whole wide world!"

"Well, this is where you're gonna get it," SpongeBob replied, pointing directly ahead into the mountains beyond the carnival. "Just keep looking, pal! One present coming right up!"

"Ooooooo!" Patrick said, clapping his hands together with glee. "My valentine is coming!"

While Patrick was distracted, SpongeBob turned away and slipped his shell-phone out of his square pants. "SpongeBob to Sandy," he whispered. "Come in, Sandy! Urgent!"

Back at the balloon, Sandy was in the middle of a terrific brawl! Dozens of chattering scallops were swarming around the two-fisted squirrel and her rich chocolate valentine!

"Sandy to SpongeBob, I got my ox in a ditch over here! Hi-yah!" she cried, placing a well-aimed karate chop at the chin of a hungry scallop. "I'm way off course!"

"How far?" SpongeBob asked. Patrick was

growing more and more restless.

"Beats me, but being lost ain't the problem! These scrunchy ol' scallops are eatin' the balloon!" Sandy replied, punching another shellfish away. "They're everywhere! It's only a matter of time before—"

With those words, one of the scallops broke through Sandy's defenses and bit down hard into the chocolate balloon!

"Aw, shoot!" Sandy groaned.

Air came rushing out of the hole, and the valentine began to drift to the bottom of the ocean.

"We're goin' down, SpongeBob!" Sandy cried. "Switch to Plan B! Switch to Plan B! Sandy over and out!"

"No, Sandy, no!" SpongeBob said. "There is no Plan B! No Plan B!"

The shell-phone was dead. SpongeBob was on his own!

chapter seven

SpongeBob put his shell-phone away before turning to Patrick.

"I don't see it, SpongeBob!" Patrick said in a high-pitched voice. "Do *you* see it? 'Cause I *don't* see it!"

"Uh, well, gee Patrick . . . you know how sometimes you plan something special and things just don't work out?" SpongeBob said nervously.

"No! I don't!" Patrick said, sweat starting to

bead on his forehead. He wiped his brow and turned to SpongeBob. "Holy mackerel! Is it hot up here or what?"

Before SpongeBob could answer the question, Patrick stood up in the Ferris wheel seat. The car shifted, nearly tossing SpongeBob out from beneath the safety restraint bar.

Patrick ripped off his new white T-shirt and threw away the pieces. "Gahhhaa!" he screamed. Scared of falling, SpongeBob tried to wedge himself into the far corner of the Ferris wheel seat.

Patrick began to jump up and down, chanting, "Valentine! Valentine! Valentine!"

From the base of the mighty Ferris wheel to the highest point where SpongeBob and Patrick were perched, the entire carnival ride began to squeak and moan.

SpongeBob's body flapped like a flag in the breeze as he hung on to the safety bar.

"Yaaaaaaah!" he screamed! "Patrick, stop!"

Patrick shook the Ferris wheel even harder. "Val-en-tine! Val-en-tine! Val-en-tine!" he chanted.

"Wait, Patrick, hold it!" SpongeBob cried in sheer terror. He freed one of his hands and waved it at his rampaging pal. "Here it is! I've got your valentine present!"

Patrick froze and turned to look at SpongeBob.

SpongeBob smiled, waggling his fingers. "Eh, hah-ha-ha-ha!" he tittered.

Patrick sat down, and the Ferris wheel stopped shaking. The starfish furrowed his brow and peered at SpongeBob's outstretched hand.

"What's that?" he asked.

"A handshake!" SpongeBob said in his best salesmanlike pitch. "A *friendly* handshake!"

One of Patrick's eyes twitched as he slumped in his seat. He took a deep breath, and then said in a calm voice. "A handshake? *That's* the big gift? You got me a *HANDSHAKE*?!"

SpongeBob reached over and grabbed Patrick's hand and shook it vigorously. "Not just any ordinary ol' handshake! A *friendly* handshake! Happy Valentine's Day!"

As if on cue, the Ferris wheel clanked, and began to lower them to the ground.

Patrick looked at his hand. He didn't say a word, even as his face deflated in disappointment.

Patrick was *not* happy.

"Come on!" SpongeBob said, trying to change the subject as he led Patrick down the boardwalk to the next attraction. "There's lots more stuff to see!"

First there was a visit to the Buddy Bounce,

where SpongeBob happily bounced to and fro like a weightless astronaut on the moon. Patrick also bounced, but his gloomy expression didn't change.

Next was the Wild Mollusk Roller Coaster. SpongeBob and Patrick sat in the front seat and raced around the tracks. SpongeBob screamed and waved, while Patrick stared at his hand and frowned.

Finally, hoping the sights and sounds of the Tiki Fun House would cheer Patrick up, SpongeBob led his friend into the hall of mirrors. SpongeBob giggled as their reflections twisted in comical ways, but Patrick wasn't paying any attention.

SpongeBob sat down on a bench and sighed. How could he make things up to his disappointed pal?

chapter eight

Patrick sat, rubbed his pink chin thoughtfully, and turned to look at SpongeBob.

"I've been thinking," Patrick said in a monotone voice. "At first, a handshake doesn't seem like much, but really, it's the thought that counts."

A tall pink eel slithered up to the bench. She was holding a large heart-shaped box. "Hey, SpongeBob! I just wanted to thank you for this lovely box of chocolates!"

SpongeBob smiled at the eel. "No problem, Fran!"

Patrick frowned, and then continued to speak: "I mean, even though I was expecting more—"

A green fish with an armful of roses strolled up and waved to SpongeBob. "Thanks for the roses, SpongeBob! Happy Valentine's Day!"

SpongeBob sunk down on the bench. "Uh, you too, Dave! Glad you liked them."

Patrick tightened his jaw muscles, and went on, "And not that it matters that we've been friends for so long—"

A blue fish in a yellow dress rode up on a bicycle and stopped next to the bench. She leaned over and said, "Hey, SpongeBob! Thanks for the bike!"

SpongeBob pulled his head down into the collar of his white dress shirt like a

turtle disappearing into his shell.

The blue fish elbowed Patrick and said, "Can you believe this guy? I just met him this morning!"

As she pedaled away, Patrick continued: "So, as I was saying—"

"Excuse me," a new voice said. "Do you guys have the time?"

Patrick whirled on the interloper and grabbed him by the shoulders! Hefting the unlucky guppy over his head, the furious starfish hurled him into the midst of the Happy Valentine's Ring Toss game.

"Yoooaaggghah!" Patrick cried. "PATRICK NEEDS LOVE TOO!"

Patrick beat his chest like a gorilla and ran down the boardwalk into the midst of the carnival, crying in anger and disappointment.

"Oh, no! This is all my fault!" SpongeBob

cried, chasing after his friend. "I've got to try and stop him!"

"AAROOOOOO!" Patrick bellowed. "Where's MY love? Where's the love for Patrick?"

No one was safe! Not the ticket taker, not the soda-pop girl, not even the poor slob wearing the giant red valentine costume and entertaining the kiddies!

"It's an art to have a heart!" the costumed fish sang. "Won't you be mine here in the brine?"

"Yay!" the little fishes replied, wiggling their fins. "We love you, Heartie!"

"Arrrgh! I defy you, heart man!" Patrick screamed, bounding up and scattering the children like scaly bowling pins.

"Run! It's a monster!" the kids cried, fleeing for safety.

Patrick ripped the bright red suit off the poor

entertainer's shoulders, leaving a confused actor standing in his underwear!

A siren began to wail. Over the carnival loudspeaker system, an announcer warned, "Attention, everyone! There's a chubby pink starfish on the loose!"

The panic was on! Everyone ran for the exits! No one wanted to cross an angry starfish!

Especially one that had undergone such a terrible transformation: Patrick's color had changed from pink to purple and his eyes were bloodshot. Pumped up with anger and disappointment, he was now ten times as strong as the average starfish!

He was also ten times as angry.

"Unhappy Valentine's Day, everyone!" Patrick yelled as he ran toward the Swing for Two ride. There were dozens of pairs of swings attached to a tall red-and-white striped pole, and perched on the top was a giant, blinking red heart!

"Heart on stick must die!" Patrick snarled. He wrapped his arms around the base of the pole and strained with all his might to pull it up from the ground!

chapter nine

"GWARRR!" Patrick yelled as he struggled to wreck the swing ride.

"No, Patrick! Don't do it!" SpongeBob cried from a safe distance. "I'll make it up to you, I promise!"

Patrick growled, grunted, and pulled as hard as he could, but the mammoth pole wouldn't budge. At last he fell on his butt and put his head in his hands.

"Rooo!" he moaned sadly. "Rooooo!"

A little girl approached Patrick to see if he was okay. She was carrying a red heart-shaped lollipop.

Patrick looked up, spied the lollipop, and once again cried out, "Heart on stick must die!"

Snatching the candy away from the child, the starfish bit the heart-shaped candy off at the tip, chomping and drooling with delight!

SpongeBob stamped his foot. Taking candy from kids was a definite no-no!

"Patrick!" he scolded. "How could you?"

The starfish spun around, his eyes bulging in their sockets and his mouth smeared with red sticky candy. "Mwalughmuhgum!" Patrick snarled. All friendliness was gone, leaving nothing behind but a scaly monster!

"Yikes!" SpongeBob squeaked, fleeing to hide in the midst of the gathering crowd. He was hoping for safety in numbers.

Patrick stood, his arms outstretched, and began to stomp toward the onlookers.

One step forward by Patrick.

One step back by the crowd.

SpongeBob kept his head down, hoping Patrick wouldn't see him.

Patrick picked up the pace and moved closer, his beady eyes seeking out his spongy yellow target.

As one, the crowd shuffled away, trying to maintain their distance from the frustrated starfish. But there was nowhere left for them to go. Patrick had backed them to the end of the dock!

"GRAAAAAH!" the angry starfish yelled. "Give me SpongeB-o-b-b-b!"

The crowd promptly tossed SpongeBob out on his nose.

"Ha-ha-ha-ha-ha!" SpongeBob laughed nervously as he looked up at Patrick. "How's it going?"

"You broke my heart!" Patrick said, waving a fist. "Now, I'm gonna break something of yours!"

SpongeBob got up to his feet and stuck his hands deep in his pockets. "Okay, Patrick," he said sadly. "I know I deserve this!"

"That's right!" Patrick cried. "You deserve it all, 'Mr. Greatest Bestest Most Fantabulous Valentine's Day Present Ever!'"

SpongeBob gestured to the crowd gathered behind him. "I might deserve it, but do they?" Everyone smiled nervously. A few waved their wallets. One lady winked and blew a kiss.

Patrick wasn't buying it. He stomped his foot and bellowed, "They didn't get me anything EITHER!"

A torrent of chocolates, valentines, and presents landed at Patrick's feet.

"Nope!" Patrick said stomping through the pile of gifts. "It's too late for that now! For *all* of you!"

But then, as the angry starfish advanced on the helpless crowd, a new sound rang out across the carnival! A humming noise, like that of a hundred sets of teeth all chattering at once, echoed over the boardwalk!

"Yee-hah! Git along, little shellfish!" Sandy cried, riding atop a repaired, but still intact, heart-shaped chocolate balloon with pink marshmallow starfish on the sides!

With one hand, she cracked a whip. In the other, she held the reins for the now-tamed scallops who were pulling her along!

"Yay! Woo-hoo! Sandy's here!" SpongeBob called. "Valentine's Day is saved!"

chapter ten

"Gallop, you scallops!" Sandy called, expertly maneuvering the balloon. Dropping the reins, she freed the scallops, and the chocolate valentine landed without a sound behind Patrick.

SpongeBob was so excited, he could hardly speak. "Look Patrick! It's here! It's here!" he called. "The best valentine in the whole wide world is right behind you!"

"Su-u-r-r-re it is."

"Really!" SpongeBob replied, pointing at the balloon. "See?!"

Patrick crossed his arms and gave SpongeBob a sarcastic grin. "You must think I'm pretty dumb, huh?"

"YES!" the crowd replied in unison.

"Well, I'm not!" Patrick sneered. "I know this is just another trick!"

"But I'm telling you the present is right there!" SpongeBob urged. "Turn around!"

"Nuh-uh!"

SpongeBob stepped closer to Patrick and tried to move him, but the hefty starfish would not budge. "Come on, Patrick!" he begged. "Just turn around!"

"Yeah! Turn around!" someone in the crowd called.

"Nothing doing!" Patrick replied.

"Turn around! Turn around! Turn around!

Turn around!" the crowd chanted.

Patrick was firm. "No, I won't! No, I won't!" he chanted back.

"Turn around! Turn around!"

"You can't make me!"

"Turn! Turn! Turn!"

Patrick hiked up his Bermuda shorts and frowned. "I'm only gonna say this once, and I'm not gonna say it again, so pay attention!" he said. "I am not, I repeat, *NOT,* going to turn around for any reason . . . *EVER!*"

"Howdy, Patrick!" Sandy called from the top of the balloon.

Patrick turned around with a big smile and waved.

"Hi, Sandy!" he replied, before his mouth fell open and hit the wood of the dock with a *ka-clunk.*

There, before his fevered eyes, was the

biggest, most coolest, chocolatey valentine ever! Just like SpongeBob had promised!

"Duh-muh-ba-duh-guh—," Patrick babbled in shock.

SpongeBob slapped him on the back. "Happy Valentine's Day, Patrick!"

"Yay! Yay! Mine! Valentine!" Patrick called as he ran over and embraced the chocolate balloon.

"Awwwwww!" the crowd said, relieved.

Scrambling to get his arms around the balloon, Patrick pressed his face into the chocolate. The valentine smelled delicious! Patrick just had to take one bite!

"Hey, SpongeBob! Is this solid chocolate?" the starfish called, before sinking his teeth into the present.

"Patrick, NO!" SpongeBob cried, but his warning came too late.

The balloon burst with a loud "POP!" covering the entire carnival in a gooey candy mess! Sticky pieces of chocolate valentine and hunks of pink marshmallow were everywhere.

After a moment, Patrick lifted his head. His face was smeared with candy.

SpongeBob's feet appeared nearby, followed by the rest of his body as he wiggled out from under the burst balloon. His head and clothes were coated in chocolate.

Up to their necks in goo, Patrick and SpongeBob looked at each other.

Patrick grinned. "Awwwww, gee, SpongeBob," he said. "You really didn't have to get me anything!"

We